Stand Still Youth Pt 1

As youth in this world we all know that you here for difference Missions to complete. So in everything you do according to your calling or your gift you're given by the almighty God.

when God created man he said lets make man in our own image and let them have domain and subdue also multiply.

h

' l

f

h

d h

d l

d

So as youth you're living forgetting what God has declared in your life's and that's where you find yourself in an wrong race because you're trying to join a race which it is not yours so that's where your life will not determine how attachments or future opportunities will be.

So as youth you need to know that you're responsible for your future and how you need to live like or how you want your world to be like because according to the word of God we're the gods f h

ld

'

h

b h

l

h

d

l

of this world we're given the power by the almighty God to rule and overthrow the world .

Life as youth must not control you or the world because the power is in you and anyone who does not use the power is useless so you need to show the real you through Jesus Christ our Lord and personal saviour.

fi

d

h

l d

d

l

But first you need to accept him as your lord and personal saviour and let him forgive you all your sins because of what he did in the cross and his resurrection and he shall baptise you with fire and the holy Ghost.

So when you have Jesus in you that's where you'll starts to have a good life and experience the kingdom of God because of his righteousness we live and move peacefully in a way that h

h h ll

d

l

h ll l

b

everything you touch shall prosper and miracles shall also be your potion.

So you must always stand still with God in whatever you're doing life because without God you always forget who you're and find yourself being in a Position where by you all start doing the things of this world and for people like that they are out of the glory of God.

h

l

h

d

So as youth you must always remain in your position where God has placed you in because there's a purpose of the placement so stand still with the word of God so that the world must not control you by your own mistakes or forgetting the most important things.

The life and the world we're in need you as youth because there's the reason why God has placed you here on earth and as k

h

h

f lfill

d f

we know everyone has his or own assignment to fulfill and for you to fulfill it you need the help of God who sent you…

When you know your assignment you will always want to reach your destiny and if you you don't know your purpose is this world that's where you find yourself in a bad environment or group of people where you're completely lost and always having problem in life..

b

h

d l

d h ' l

You must remember that God loves you and he's love is unconditional and he want you to rejoice in his name and live in a better way in righteous because there's know one who's perfect more than someone else you're all the Same ,the difference is that you don't have the same assignment to complete until to your destiny.

God is your refuge and strength, an ever-present help in trouble.

Therefore you must not fear, though the earth give way and the f ll

h h

f h

h

h

mountains fall into the heart of the sea, though its waters roar and foam and the mountains quake with their surging.

Trust in the LORD with all your heart, and lean not on your own understanding; in all your ways acknowledge Him, and He shall direct your paths"

Don't worry about temptation no temptation has overtaken you that is not common to man. God is faithful, and he will not let b

k d b

d

b l

b

h h

h

you be tempkted beyond your ability, but with the temptation he will also provide the way of escape, that you may be able to endure it.

Always stand still with God as youth of this world so you can make the world to rejoice in the Lord because of what he has done in the cross for us to have internal life to live and worship God in his kingdom of heaven.

f h l

d h

l

Because of his love we must rejoice in it and show our love to other as the Lord did by sending his Only begotten son to us.so because of his love we are able to settle in the house of the Lord only by the love which has no measurement.

The Word of God contains a treasure trove of Bible verses about love. You'll find passages that speak of romantic love, brotherly love, and divine love.

h l

d

d

h

d l d

h

That love your enemies, do good to them, and lend to them without expecting to

get anything back. Then your reward will be great, and you will be sons of the
Most High, because he is kind to the ungrateful and wicked.

Love is patient, love is kind. It does not envy, it does not boast, it is not proud. It
is not rude, it is not self-seeking, it is not easily angered, it keeps no record of
wrongs. Love does not delight in evil but rejoices with the truth. It always
protects, always trusts, l

h

l

f l

h

always hopes, always perseveres. Love never fails. But where there are
prophecies, they will cease; where there are tongues, they will be stilled; where
there is knowledge, it will pass away.

There is no fear in love. But perfect love drives out fear, because fear has to do
with punishment. The one who fears is not made perfect in love. We love
because he first loved us.

h

h

k

h l

h

l d d

h l f

This is how we know what love is: Jesus Christ laid down his life for us. And we
ought to lay down our lives for our brothers. If anyone has material possessions
and sees his brother in need but has no pity on him, how can the love of God be

in him? Dear children, let us not love with words or tongue but with actions and in truth.

So that's how as you're a youth you must act and show love to one another as the Lord does don't hate or be jealous of one h

b

lf

d

l

d

another ,just be yourself and consecrate on your goal and assignment untill your destiny.

When God created humans, he designed us to live in families.

Family relationships, therefore, are important to God. Even the church, the universal body of believers, is called the family of God.

f h

d

h

h

d h

Honor your father and your mother, as the LORD your God has commanded you, so that you may live long and that it may go well with you in the land the LORD your God is giving you.

The Bible says in the book of :John 15:12-17

"This is my commandment, that you love one another as I have loved you.

Greater love has no one than this, that someone lay down his life for his friends. You are my friends if you do what I command you. No longer do I call you servants, for the servant d

k

h h

d

b

h

ll d

does not know what his master is doing; but I have called you friends, for all that I have heard from my Father I have made known to you. You did not choose me, but I chose you and appointed you that you should go and bear fruit and that your fruit should abide, so that whatever you ask the Father in my name, he may give it to you.

Our earthly relationships are important to the Lord. God the Father ordained the institution of marriage and designed for us l

h f

l

h h

'

lk

b

f

d h

to live within families. Whether we're talking about friendships, dating relationships, marriages, families, or dealings between brothers and sisters in Christ, the Bible has a great deal to say about our relationships with one another.

Praise be to the God and Father of our Lord Jesus Christ! In his great mercy he has given us new birth into a living hope through the resurrection of Jesus Christ from the dead, and into an inheritance that can never perish, spoil or fade--kept in heaven f

h h

h f h

h ld d b

d'

l h

for you, who through faith are shielded by God's power until the coming of the salvation that is ready to be revealed in the last time.

For God so loved the world that he gave his one and only Son, that whoever believes in him shall not perish but have eternal life and as you a youth must always stand still with the word of the Lord almighty God.

l

k

h

f

l f b

You must also know the power of position in your life because it's has etymology from the Latin word *positio* meaning the act or fact of placing , situation, position.it also mean proper place occupied by a person or thing.

This gives us the idea that there is a conductive state for a thing or person to be positioned that either makes it or the right place for it or the person to function with full capacity.

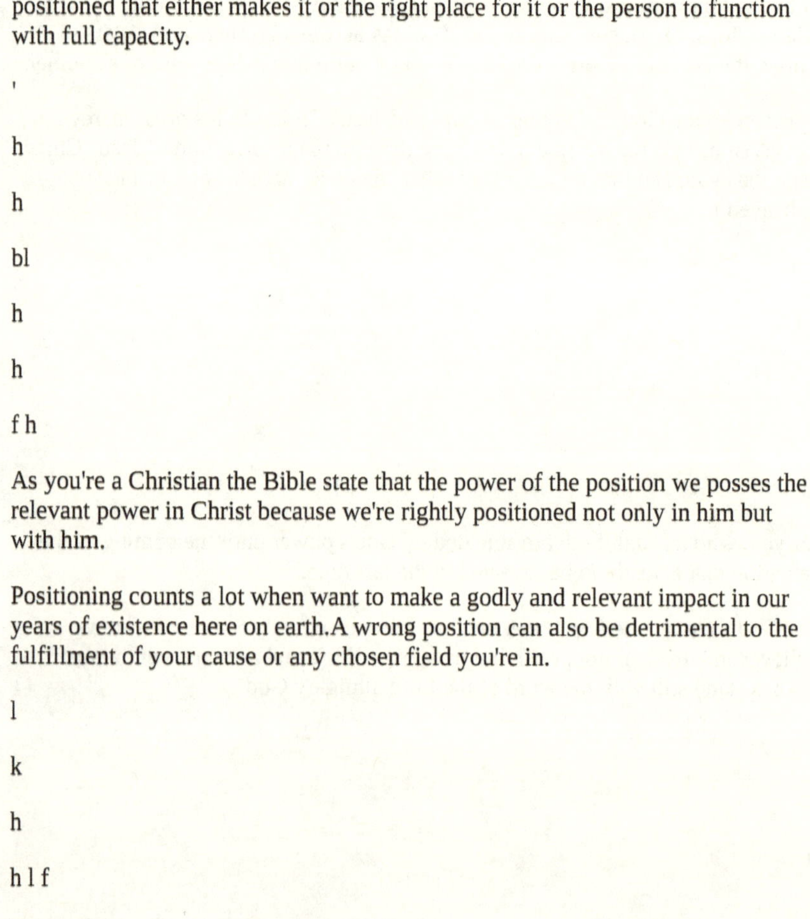

As you're a Christian the Bible state that the power of the position we posses the relevant power in Christ because we're rightly positioned not only in him but with him.

Positioning counts a lot when want to make a godly and relevant impact in our years of existence here on earth. A wrong position can also be detrimental to the fulfillment of your cause or any chosen field you're in.

You must also know that as a youth life is more spiritual than physical and understanding this gives you another undeniable great outcome.

This brings you to the idea of how you are powerful positioned in terms of our human makeup. The Bible makes it clear that before God created man there was an agreement among the Trinity .

'

l b

h

l

l

As you're a spiritual being,the supernatural is your natural identity.if God is a spirit and you are formed according to his nature or the nature of the trinity it's clear that our first and foremost nature is of a spirit being

So you must understand that you're operating on the supernatural realm of positioning in your life don't forget that the importance of it because the position you're in is so important and relevant to in good way.

h

l

d

ll

d fi h f

As youth you must always stand still and fight for your victory in this world you're in sometimes you may think that the people don't like you but you must understand you're a stranger in this world you belong in heaven

So don't give up when you see people tying to bring you down because of achievement and prosperity just keep on running your own race and focus on your assignment and build your self in Christ until.

f

h ll

h '

b

Do not fear any challenges that's comes your way because those Challenges are there to make and rise you and push to your next level of life or your destination .

As the Bible says "fear not for the Lord your God is with you" so there's no need to have the fear in you for everything that comes your way because you VB won't see what God has planned for you only just believe and trust in the Lord with all your heart.

b

l

d

h

l f

Sometimes you may be planning to do so something in your life that will also help other and you don't know how to start or something may be blocking but don't give there's is God who is the starter and finisher of everything so just bow down and pray Because if you give up you'll be blocking yourself to your self and the devil may be behind that so that you can not achieve anything in your life and see nothing moving.

l

h

d

d h

h

'

l

Also as a Christian you must understand that there's no longer you operating but the spirit of the Lord that dwells in you. That helps you understand and figure out everything you wanna do to complete your assignment.

So when you fill like there's something you wanna achieve in your journey just believe is part of your assignment and if if it's part of it that's means that that the plan or voice of the Lord showing you.

b

h

'

h

h k

h

Remember that you've Christ in you who knows whatever you want in life so stand still , believe in the Lord do not moving according to the world says but according to the Lord commandments.

Sometimes you may think the life you're living is not God enough and things are not moving in a way you want but understand that that ways of the Lord are not the same as yours .

h

d h

h

l f

d

So sometimes the Lord has the greater picture in your life and he knows the future and how it would be like, so that's where you need to trust in the Lord and believe that all things work according for your own good.

You just have to know that everything that is in your way you will over come then because by the the blood if Jesus you where set free nothing can shake your faith there's a loving God in you.

l f

h

d

h

f h

d b

In life as youth you need to have faith in God because we thought faith you're nothing in this world because everything that we do is according to faith.

The Bible uses the words faith and belief or believe interchangeably. Eternal life is received by grace through faith.

Faith is the victory that overcomes the world and without faith it is impossible to please God

h

h h

b l

d

h

d h

f

h

So Through him you believe in God, who raised him from the dead and glorified him, and so your faith and hope are in God.

For everyone born of God overcomes the world. This is the victory that has overcome the world, even your faith.

Now faith is being sure of what you hope for and certain of what you do not see. This is what the ancients were commended for.

By faith you understand that the universe was formed at God's d

h

h

d

f h

command, so that what is seen was not made out of what was visible

Let you fix your eyes on Jesus, the author and perfecter of your faith, who for the joy set before him endured the cross, scorning its shame, and sat down at the right hand of the throne of God.

The Bible says in John 14:12

I tell you the truth, anyone who has faith in me will do what I h

b

d

ll d

h

h

h

have been doing. He will do even greater things than these, because I am going to the Father

So you are able to greater than everything that Jesus did so you're already given the power in your hands you just have to stand still and show the real you in Christ .

In Second Corinthians 4:16-18

"So we do not lose heart. Though our outer man is wasting lf

b

d d

b d

h l h

away, our inner self is being renewed day by day. For this light momentary affliction is preparing for us an eternal weight of glory beyond all comparison, as we look not to the things that are seen but to the things that are unseen. For the things that are seen are tranhsient, but the things that are unseen are eternal."

Always listen to the voice of the Lord because it gives life and victory don't allow the devil to lie to you because he only come l

d k ll

l

h

d

d

'

to lie and kill so always stay in the Lord present a d Don't give you on God because the wont give up on you he's able Don't try to go in the spirit because you're already there . so the moment you try to move in the spirit you're moving out of the spirit,so you must know that as you received Jesus you have moved from the flesh to the spirit.

'

d

d k

l d

b

h

Don't try to use your own wisdom and knowledge because they are foolish and they only course destruction from you and your life so always the Lord to give you the wisdom and knowledge for your life.

As you stand still you must always respect your purpose and gift also calling because they came from God who loves and that's where we must always respect it.

l

ll

h

f h

d

l

d

Always allow the spirit of the Lord to control you and move you to your destiny because he's there to help you and comfort you and raise you in Christ.

Always have time to worship God everytime when you're free because that will show how you love him and how you need need him and blessings shall flow you all the time.

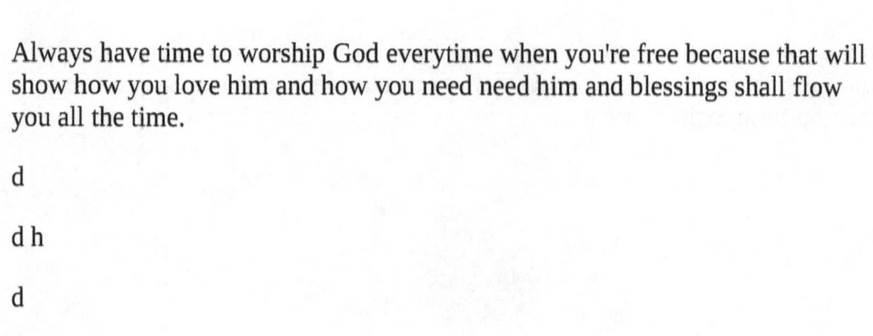

d

d h

d

ll

l

You must understand that God will never put you in a place without ba reason and you must always have fellowship with God study the word of God so that you must have knowledge of him.

Sometimes you may need patients because God only need you to understand that in every he does not do according to the ways of the world but according to his glory.

l

b

dl

h

ld b

h

bl

'

Always be Godliness in this world because the Bible says we're the gods if this world and you must understand that as you're then show it and never let anything to bring you down.

So as youth you must always stand still and always make show you don't fall down from your Christianity and meditate all the time so the word must stay in you and give you life.

h

h

h d

ll

h d

l

d

Another thing is that do not allow the devil to deceive you because you'll found your self in a wrong position of life and it all affect your spirituality and religion…

Because what he wants is to make you think you're nothing in this world feeding you with lies and the more you loose your faith in God because of focusing on your problems the more depression and anxiety will follow you d l

d

l

d b

b

h

h h

And also do not let pride be in you because those who have pride are the followers of the devil , don't allow evil spirits to control you in to something you're not , you're the child of the most high we live by faith and love.

Everytime in your life do not be angry like the Bible says Revelation 12:12

[12]Be glad then, O heavens, and you who are in them. But there is trouble for the earth and the sea: because the Evil One has d

b

h

h k

l d

h

come down to you, being very angry, having the knowledge that he has but a short time.

So if you're always angry you're in the compass of the devil because he has deceive by bringing challenges and situation where by you even loose hope and think about that the Lord has forgotten you but stand still in faith as youth..

l

k

h

h d

l

h

f

d

l l k h

Also know that the devil is the persecute of God people like the Bible says in

Revelation 12:13

[13]And when the dragon saw that he was forced down to the earth, he made cruel attacks on the woman who gave birth to the male child.

So this shows as that whenever you see people attacking you because of something you did or have just know that is the devil h

lf d

ll

h

h h

him self do not allow him to overcome you with his persecutions He's also accuse the brethren by all means because he knows you're the child of the most high ,when you see people accusing you understand that is the deceivement of the devil him self.

Understand that if you're poor in the physical you're rich in the spirit and allow things

l

d

d h

h d

l

h f h

f l

h

bl

Also understand that the devil is the father of lies the Bible says in

John 8:44

[44]You are the children of your father the Evil One and it is your pleasure to do his desires. From the first he was a taker of life; and he did not go in the true way because there is no true thing in him. When he says what is false, it is natural to him, for he is false and the father of what is false.

d ' b d

d b h l

f h d

l b

h l d

So don't be deceived by the lies of the devil be strong in the lord and always pay attention to to the sprit of the lord that will guide you unto your righteousness..

You must also know that the devil does not know anything about you all he does he searches information in you by what you always do ,so you must always be glad in the lord wether in challenges or bad situation.

h

d

d h

h

l

So as youth you Must understand that the only way to survive in this world is through Jesus Christ our Lord and personal saviour he's the one who will protect you against any situation you'll face in life

There's something that you must know about God is that he can do everything , nothing is impossible to him ,so don't lose hope when things are not going well "as the Bible says all things d

d" h '

h

h

according to our own good" that's mean that what ever happened in your life for the better…

Always know the times of God ,that will help you to find what you need and to exercise your relationship with God this are the times of God "space" you need to be in a space where God has placed you for you to have something in God l

h

'

"

" h

d

d h

h

d

Also there's is "Time" where you must understand that the Lord has his on time don't expect to have something or to see some on your on time also because the things of the spirit are not the same as of this world.

In the spirit there's so much speed and that speed according to us it depends on the Revolution we have as Christian's,so you must understand stand in what ever you do in the Lord there's always speed .

h

d

d h

h

h

d

As youth we must understand that we have the anointing and the star In you do not give up on your star you must understand how the system of God works and every thing happens in your life God already knows just move by what God is saying .

The kingdom of God has two things and they are believer's and non-believer's and as you're are believer you always face the non-believer's and that's need you as youth to stand still in the Lord always in faith and worshipping the Lord as always.

'

h

f h

ld

'

h

h

d

You're the CEO of this world,you're given the authority and we must use it in this world that's why In life we'll have to dream big and never give up, let us run our own race until we reach our destination in life...

Don't forget who you're in the Lord and also don't forget the love he has for you trust in him let the spirit of the Lord take over you'll see things happening in your life..

h '

h

l

k

d

k

l d

That's something you must always know and acknowledge about the revolution about Jesus who died for as in the cross and rose again..

You must know that we don't do things for God , because what we're is from God he lives in us,in him we live and you can't do anything or something for God.

h

h f ll

d

f

When you receive Jesus you receive his fullness and as for you must have a personal relationship with God so that you must understand that this of the kingdom of God You must also understand that the name of "jesus" is so powerful like never before even demons trimble when they here that name because it so powerful..

h

d

h

f

d

h

Why you pray and you say the name of Jesus and nothing happened it is because of the the revolution you have about Jesus Christ and that how the name of Jesus will work for you so that you must always standing still.

Christianity is about understanding the principal God you must have a personal counter with Jesus,it important to have a personal counter with him

l

k

h

d h

d

You must also know that Jesus is God they are one and Jesus was not born in the new testament he was the there before the earth and the heavens he is in the Trinity..

In the old testament he was the father but in the new testament he was the son and when he goes in the heaven he was the spirit

h

bl

h

The Bible says in John 8:56-58

[56]Your father Abraham was full of joy at the hope of seeing my day: he saw it

and was glad.

[57]Then the Jews said to him, You are not fifty years old; have you seen Abraham?

[58]Jesus said to them, Truly I say to you, Before Abraham came into being, I am.

h

h

h

h

b h

h

d

It shows that Jesus was there when Abraham was there and Abraham also saw Jesus..

Sometimes you must understand the what the name of Jesus means look at the Bible it says

Revelation 19:13

[13]And he is clothed in a robe washed with blood: and his name is The Word of God.

l

h

h

f

h

d f

d d

So it also show us the name of Jesus means the word of God do to call the name of Jesus you must be powerful in the word of God which bis the Bible you carry everyday..

As youth must also developed a relationship with God you must respect the word of God which is the bible and it is the Ark of God it is compaliation we live it and it is a reality…

h

'

d ff

f k

h d

d l

There's a different of knowing Jesus you hard and also Jesus you have a personal relationship with because it will help you to sustain the things of the kingdom of God So as youth you must always be in the word because it is a strong tower that will help you to reach your destiny and you will get there by only reading the bible and meditating on it everyday..

h

l

d

d

d

As a youth you must also pray every day do not pass a day not praying because prayer is the food of your spirit so you must always have time for God and talk to him in problem and when things are good.

REPENT...

Repent means to change physical and also to grow spiritually by fearing God and as you have repent you must always do the first k b h

h

f

d l

h

h

d f

d

work by having hunger for God also hearing the word of God also studying the Bible.

Also you must always sacrifice everything you have to the Lord because of his glory and also have the love of Jesus in you because it is unconditional it can be measured by any scale.

You must also understand that repent does not mean to say forgive me Lord but to stop everything and fear the Lord and b

d

f

d

d b

d f

being ready to confess your sin and and being ready for persucation for Christ because for you to live is Christ and to die is gain.

Beloved,

Let's start with a quote from Ephesians 1:7.

h

d

(d l

d

l

) h

h

In Him we have redemption (deliverance and salvation) through His blood, the remission (forgiveness) of our offenses (shortcomings and trespasses), in accordance with the riches and the generosity of His gracious favor Eph. 1:7 (AMP) You're not forgiven according to your sin but according to God's riches and glory. So to know how forgiven you are, just find out how much is his riches and glory. Your forgiveness is boundless, immeasurable, and infinite. You have been boundlessly, bl

d fi

l f

l

k

ll

immeasurably, and infinitely forgiven. Until you know very well that you have been forgiven, you will continually struggle with sin, guilt, and condemnation.

The feeling of guilt and condemnation come because people do not know that they have been forgiven. And that feeling of guilt and condemnation is what drags people back to sin. That's why Jesus refused to condemn the woman caught in adultery. He h

h

f f

d

h

h

d

gave her the gift of no-condemnation so that she can go and have the power not to sin anymore.

The revelation of the forgiveness of ALL your sins will empower you to live far above sin. You struggle with sin because you still think God has not forgiven you and he is on his way to punish you. This kind of thinking is the very reason why people keep struggling with sin even when they do not want to. Peter said l f l

d

h b

h

h

f

h

h

people fail to do right because they have forgotten that their sins are forgiven (2Pet.1:7-9).

The forgiveness of our sins is what removes us from satan's dominion and places us far above all principalities and powers.

What took us there was Adam's sin but now that Christ has fully satisfied the claims of justice. We can now live free forever from satan and his evil works.

REPENT PRAYER:

Dear heavenly Father, I trust you as the only living God who will live eternally. I understand that I cannot be in harmony with you until I have confessed my faith in your Son Jesus Christ.

Therefore, I confess my faith in him today. I believe that Jesus is your true and only Son sent to save the world. I confess my sins and repent from them. I declare Jesus Christ as the Lord of my life, and I promise to devote my total life to him from today.

h

f

d

f h

l b l

h

Since I have confessed my faith in Jesus, I strongly believe that I am now your child – and I am heavenly bound! Praise be to your holy name for making me heavenly worthy. Praise be to you today, and praises be to your forever!

Amen.

Stand still youth the Lord is with you rejoice in him..

(

d

)

(Word Count: 4905)

This document is generated from JotterPad.